Alligator Swamp

by Sean Taylor

illustrated by Neil Chapman

Contents

PEARSON

Longman

Text © Sean Taylor 2003
Series editors: Martin Coles and Christine Hall

PEARSON EDUCATION LIMITED
Edinburgh Gate
Harlow
Essex CM20 2JE
England

www.longman.co.uk

First published 2003
ISBN 0582 79612 1

Illustrated by Neil Chapman

With thanks to Murilo Reis who took us into the swamp, and to "Uncle"
Carlos for his help with the research.

Dedicated to Adriana, with love

Printed in Great Britain by Scotprint, Haddington

The publishers' policy is to use paper manufactured from sustainable forests.

1 Fazenda Arara

"You're now in one of the wildest places anywhere in the world," nodded Luis, picking up his bag. Mum went first, and I followed. It was midnight and only a few days before Christmas, but, as we stepped off the plane, the air felt like a heater blowing in our faces.

"Phoow!" said Mum, fanning herself with the in-flight magazine.

Across the tarmac was a sign saying 'WELCOME TO CORUMBÁ: HEART OF THE PANTANAL'. As we walked towards it I could feel mosquitoes buzzing around my eyes.

We were met by a short, brown-faced man with big shoulders and a moustache about the size of a scrubbing brush. He adjusted his tatty, leather hat and shook hands with each of us. Luis said his name was Alberto and he was the farm manager. His fingers were heavy and thick and, when he bent down to pick up our bags, I noticed six shotgun cartridges tucked into his belt.

He dropped our things into the back of an old pick-up truck and held open a dented door. The three of us squeezed into the front beside him, and away we drove. Propped against the dashboard on Alberto's side was a worn shotgun. I wound down the window. Outside everything smelled dusty, and it was so hot that some people were sitting outside their houses, watching TV in the street.

At first the road was good, but we left the town behind us and it began to get more and more bumpy. We didn't see any other cars. Mum put on the eyeshades from the plane and went to sleep. I stayed awake, half listening to Luis and Alberto talk.

Luis is my stepfather. He's Brazilian and he says he's very rich. I was six when he and Mum got married. At the wedding he kissed me more times than my real dad has in all my life. Mum wants me to like him. And I do – sort of. Sometimes he's funny. Once Mum's friend asked if there were hippopotamuses in Brazil and he said, "That's like asking if there are penguins in Buckingham Palace!"

Alberto kept his eyes on the road and answered Luis' questions in a deep, steady voice. The sky was full of stars and, alongside the road, I could see patches of dark water.

"This is the real Brazil!" said Luis, giving my arm a squeeze. "Can you hear the animals?"

"I can hear the mosquitoes," I said.

"Watch out. They love English blood!" grinned Luis.

We had already lived in Brazil for a year, when I was seven, in a big city on the other side of the country. I went to a Brazilian school and learned how to speak Portuguese just like the other children. So, when Luis told me we were going back to Brazil again for Christmas, the first thing I asked was if we were going to visit my old friends. He nodded and said, "But first we're going to spend three nights at a farm right across the other side of the country."

"A farm?" I asked. "What sort of farm?"

"No ordinary one," he told me. "It's called 'Fazenda Arara' and it's belonged to my family for a hundred and fifty years. It's in an amazing part of Brazil – a swamp twice the size of England. We call it the Pantanal."

Alberto stared straight ahead as we bumped towards a rickety plank bridge. Luis peered out of the window at the river.

The whole bridge seemed to sway as Alberto revved towards the middle of it. The pick-up tilted. There was no rail or anything along the side of the bridge. Luis gripped the armrest. Alberto changed gear. I caught a glimpse of the black water under us and was almost sure we were going to tip over. But the pick-up gave a bounce, and we were across, back onto the dusty road. Luis let go of the armrest and Alberto said, "That bridge is no good."

"If I'd known it was *that* bad I'd have worn my swimming trunks," said Luis.

"Are there snakes round here?" I asked.

"Big ones, anacondas," said Luis.

"I don't like snakes," I told him.

"Well, the snakes are just the first of your worries," said Luis. "You've got to watch out for the piranha fish as well."

I wrinkled up my nose. "They're the ones that eat people."

Luis gave a nod. "Their teeth are like razor blades. The water's full of them. And guess what else?"

"Hippopotamuses," I said.

"No!" said Luis flapping a hand in the air. "Stop with this hippopotamuses! You get hippopotamuses in Africa. But here we have alligators."

I turned down my mouth. "Well, I'm not going anywhere near the water."

"None of us are," said Luis, turning to Alberto. "How big are they round here, the alligators?"

Alberto raised his eyebrows. "A yellow-belly can grow almost as long as this truck."

We drove on for an hour, maybe more. Then the headlamps lit up a sign saying 'FAZENDA ARARA'. And there it was.

2 Animal Sounds

We bumped down a track towards the long, whitewashed walls of a farmhouse. Jutting out from one side was a high veranda. We pulled up underneath it, at one end of a wide yard. Alberto's wife, Lúcia, was waiting up for us. She gave a little smile and took Mum's bag as we walked in through a tall front door. Luis said Lúcia was the best cook in Brazil.

"It's not true!" she laughed. "But if you're hungry I can warm something up."

No one wanted to eat, but we were all thirsty. So Lúcia took us down a corridor into a kitchen which smelled of wood smoke and bread. She poured us cups of milk from a jug.

"Where are we exactly?" yawned Mum.

"Not far from the border between Brazil and Bolivia," said Luis. "Over a hundred kilometres from the nearest town."

"The middle of nowhere," I shrugged.

"Certainly is," nodded Luis. "The electricity's from a generator. There's no telephone. Only a radio."

Alberto sat with his shotgun propped against the back of his chair. He didn't drink or say anything. In the light I could see he had a faded tattoo on his wrist. It was a jaguar baring its teeth.

"Do you ever use that gun, Alberto?" Mum asked.

"Sometimes," said Alberto.

"He says he can shoot better than anyone in the swamp," said Lúcia, raising her eyebrows.

"It's a good shotgun," said Alberto. "It even shoots round corners."

Everyone laughed and he gave a little smile.

"Have you ever shot an alligator?" I asked.

Alberto nodded, without looking at me, then got up and said, "Excuse me. I'm tired."

"I think we all are," nodded Mum, drinking down her milk.

We were shown our rooms and Mum said she had to spray me with mosquito repellent before I went to sleep. It was horrible sticky stuff and it smelled like salad cream. She sprayed me. Then she started spraying the furniture.

"It's stinking the place out!" I complained.

"We've got to be careful," said Mum. "The book I'm reading says there are all sorts of horrible insects round here. There's one that burrows into your foot and lays eggs in your skin!"

"The windows are closed," I tutted. "Nothing can get in."

She said goodnight and left me on my own. I lifted the sheet carefully to see if there was anything in the bed that looked as though it could burrow into my feet. There wasn't, but it was so hot I didn't even feel like getting under the sheets. I just lay on top of them.

Outside animals were croaking and chirping strange little sounds, like the noises you hear in films. I don't know how long I lay there listening. Maybe I nodded off, because the next thing I knew I could hear voices somewhere outside. It seemed to be three or four men. They were talking in a hushed way, as though they didn't want to be heard. But there was something angry about them, too.

"What does it matter?" one of them asked.

"Quiet!" hissed a deep voice. It sounded like Alberto. "I don't want the visitors to know!"

They grew quieter and, for a while, I couldn't

understand what was being said. Then the deep voice whispered, "Bring your guns."

After that the voices faded away and I must have fallen asleep again. When I opened my eyes, daylight was creeping in through the shutters.

The sounds of the animals had changed. There was an amazing squawking and roaring coming from outside. My watch said ten to six. I pulled on some shorts and the Brazil football shirt Luis had bought for me.

There wasn't anyone else up. I walked down the corridor to a shadowy room with a long dining table and high windows. At one end was a heavy door. I pushed it and it swung open. The animals' sounds grew louder as I stepped out onto the veranda.

3 Mr English

All I could see was swamp. There wasn't a road, a car or a building anywhere to be seen. A river wound away into the distance. Beyond the river, grass and patches of trees stretched off. And, above it, hundreds and hundreds of birds were flying up into the sky. There were so many, they looked like coloured smoke in the sky.

I tried to imagine how far away the swamp stretched. Then a boy with bare feet and a shaved head came across the yard. There was a pair of goats sniffing at Alberto's pick-up and the boy had started to feed them from a bucket. He looked a couple of years older than me, but not much taller. He didn't see me and stood there chatting away to the goats just as though they were people. Alberto appeared, with his shotgun slung loosely over his shoulder and a coil of rope like a lasso hanging from his belt. He pointed at

the boy and said something I didn't understand.
Then he noticed me.

"Morning, Mr English," he said in his gruff voice.

"Morning!" I called back. The boy glanced up,
then turned and walked across the yard.

"Did you dream about piranha fish?" Alberto
asked.

I shook my head.

"No?" he smiled. "Well, they dreamed about
you."

I heard voices from inside the house, so I went
back in. There was a smell of fresh bread and I
found Luis sitting at the big table, drinking coffee.

"Ant," he called. "Up already?"

"I've been on the veranda," I said.

"See any hippopotamuses?"

"Just one."

"Really?" said Luis. "What was it doing?"

"Laying an egg."

Luis laughed and Mum came in.

"Morning, Anthony," she said, putting a hand
on top of my head. "I thought this place was
meant to be peaceful. I've been awake since before
six with all the racket from the animals."

"Me, too," I said. "And what was that noise in
the night?"

"What noise?" Luis asked.

"I think it was Alberto and some other men talking outside."

Luis shook his head. "Alberto went to bed before we did last night."

As he spoke Lúcia came in with a tray.

"Breakfast," she said putting the tray on the table. "Beef and rice, fresh bread and fried manioc."

I looked at the plates of strange looking food.

"Makes a change from Coco Pops," nodded Luis.

"A few breakfasts like this and you'll turn into a hippopotamus, Luis," smiled Mum.

"Ah," said Luis, "I'm used to Pantanal breakfasts. Don't forget, I used to come here all the time when my grandfather ran the farm."

"Was your grandfather a farmer?" I asked.

"An excellent farmer," said Luis, "and a great lover of wildlife. He wouldn't cut down the forest or allow wild animals to be killed on his land. That's why some of the rarest species in the Pantanal still live on this farm."

"And what about Alberto?" asked Mum. "Was he here when you were young?"

Luis nodded. "He was just one of the cowboys in those days."

"And who's that boy?" I asked.

"The lad with the shaven head?" said Luis.

"I've forgotten his name, but he was born on the farm. He was just a toddler chasing the chickens last time I was here! He must be thirteen or fourteen now. It's a sad story. His mother and father were killed in a bus crash and he ended up living with Alberto and Lúcia."

Just then Alberto appeared. He took off his leather hat and I could see the muscles in his arms like thick ropes.

"Excuse me, Mr Luis," he asked softly, "but what time do you want to go out?"

"As soon as I've eaten," nodded Luis.

Alberto turned to leave, but Luis added,

"Alberto! You weren't up in the night were you?"

Alberto's eyes fell on me. Then he looked back at Luis.

"No," he said, giving a light shake of his head.

"See," nodded Luis, pointing a finger at me, "you were dreaming."

4 Pedrinho

Luis said he and Alberto would be going out for a couple of hours.

"What about us?" asked Mum, spraying a little mosquito repellent on her legs.

"Oh, you don't want to come," he replied. "We're only going to be looking at barns and cows. I've got to try to find out why the farm isn't making as much money as it used to."

"Money, money, money," said Mum. "That's all you think about."

"Mosquitoes, mosquitoes, mosquitoes," replied Luis, bending down to give her a kiss. "That's all you think about."

Mum pointed the mosquito repellent at him. Luis backed away with his hands in the air as though it was gun. Then Mum began to spray him.

"All right!" said Luis. "I'll be back as soon as I can and I'll take you both for a drive round the swamp this afternoon!"

I heard the pick-up drive off, and went out onto the veranda again. The boy with the shaved head was painting fence posts across the yard. After a time Mum appeared. She was wearing gold-rimmed sunglasses and a bikini, and was trying to get a great big stripy sun umbrella out through the door. I helped her prop the umbrella between two chairs. Then she wanted me to put sun cream on her back. Then she asked me to take a photograph of her looking at the swamp. Then she got out her book about the Pantanal.

"It says the water round here is full of piranha fish," she said. "Did you ever see that film where a man's attacked by piranhas as he crosses a river on a horse?"

I shook my head.

"After a few moments all that's left of him and the horse is bones and red water," said Mum, looking back down at her book.

The boy had finished painting the fence posts and disappeared round the side of the farmhouse.

Mum said, "The swamp is four hundred miles wide but it's only got two main roads across it."

I raised my eyebrows. She read some more. Then she said, "And one of the commonest animals is called a capybara. It's a rodent as big as a sheep. They call it 'The Godzilla of Guinea Pigs'."

I leaned on the rail and stared into the distance for

a while, wishing I'd gone with Alberto and Luis. Then I wandered over to some wooden steps that led down to the yard.

"I think I might go down," I said.

"Well *do* be careful, Ant," said Mum, looking up. "This book says there are poisonous snakes in the grass and jaguars in the trees."

"I don't mind," I shrugged.

"Don't be stupid," said Mum angrily. Then she reached into her bag for the mosquito repellent. "And take this, just in case."

"Does it keep jaguars off as well?" I asked, sticking the spray into my back pocket.

"Probably. And put some sun cream on."

"All right." I rubbed sun cream on my legs and arms, then walked down the steps into the yard.

Underneath the veranda the goats came sniffing at my pockets, but when I stepped out into the sunshine they didn't follow. Across the yard there was a row of old outhouses. Their tin roofs clicked in the heat. One had firewood stored in it. The next looked as though it was sometimes used as a stable. I wandered round the back. There was a big square pen with two cows and two calves inside. Beyond that was a patch of wasteland with a couple of rickety goalposts stuck in the ground. The boy I'd been watching was kicking a football about on his own.

When he saw me he kicked the ball over. I kicked it back and he dribbled towards me.

"What's your name?" he called.

"Anthony," I said. "But people call me Ant."

He tried to say Anthony, but it came out more like 'auntie'. I laughed and he did too.

"All right, all right!" he said, grinning a mouthful of small, brown teeth. "How about I call you Mr English?"

"All right," I nodded.

He reached out a hand and I shook it. "Mr English, I'm Pedrinho."

He went in goal. He was good at diving for high shots, but I scored a few times by shooting hard and low. He asked how long I was staying. I told him three days.

After a time I went in goal.

"Your shirt is very beautiful," Pedrinho said, as I rolled the ball out to him.

"Luis bought it for me."

"It's the official Brazil shirt," he said with a nod. "The most expensive one."

He fired a couple more shots, then he asked, "Please, can I try your shirt?"

"All right," I said and pulled off the shirt.

"Yes," he said slipping it over his head. "Now watch out, Mr English! I am Ronaldo!"

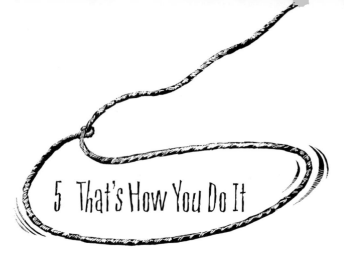

5 That's How You Do It

It was too hot to play football for very long. So we went and sat in the shade of an old tree. Pedrinho gave me my shirt back and a man came riding by on a dark horse with a dirty sheepskin under the saddle. He was thin, with a big nose and there was a thick knife tucked into the back of his jeans. He was one of the farm cowboys. Pedrinho called across and he said something back, but his accent was so strong I could hardly understand.

"We call him Toucan," said Pedrinho, as the man rode on.

"Because he's got a nose as long as a toucan's beak!" I said.

"That's it!" grinned Pedrinho.

Then I asked, "Do you go to school round here?"

"I don't go to school," Pedrinho shrugged. "Do you?"

"Yes," I nodded.

Pedrinho nodded back. Then he beamed and said, "I don't need school. I am already a professor of fishing. I fish all the time with my friends."

"Where do your friends live?"

"Over there."

He nodded up the dirt track. We both went quiet. Then Pedrinho said, "If you want you can visit my friends."

"Is it far?"

"No."

There was the sound of a car. I looked round. It was Luis and Alberto.

"We can go in the afternoon if you want."

"Okay," I said, getting to my feet and walking towards the pick-up.

Alberto leaned out of the window. "So you've met this young pest," he said.

"We were playing football."

"Mmm," winked Luis. "Who won?"

"England!" I said.

"Brazil!" said Pedrinho, at exactly the same time.

* * * * *

As we were eating lunch I told Mum and Luis that Pedrinho wanted to take me to meet his friends.

"That's good," said Luis. But Mum didn't look so sure.

"I don't like you going off without us," she said. Luis flapped a hand in the air.

"They'll be fine. Pedrinho knows this place like the back of his hand."

"What if you see a snake?" asked Mum.

"I promise I won't bite it," I told her.

I stepped back out into the sunlight and I could see Pedrinho's shaved head bobbing up and down behind the outhouses. I walked across. The ground was hard and the sun was hot on the back of my head.

He was in the cow pen, walking towards one of the calves, holding a lasso looped in six or seven coils. Alberto was leaning against the fence watching.

"All right, Mr English?" called Pedrinho, starting to swing the lasso above his head.

"Do you know how to use a lasso?" asked Alberto, nodding at me.

I shook my head.

"This young man's not bad if he puts his mind to it," growled Alberto.

"All right, all right," said Pedrinho. "This time I'll get him!"

"Let's see then," said Alberto.

The calf walked slowly along the far side of the pen. Pedrinho licked his lips, then threw the rope. The loop of it flicked through the air and landed with a *thwack* round the side of the calf's head.

Pedrinho's eyes lit up. He gripped the rope as the calf kicked for the other side of the pen. Then he strode towards the animal, leaning back, and coiling the rope round his elbow as he went.

"Better," called Alberto. "Now get her to the ground!"

Pedrinho strained at the rope, dragging the calf towards him. Then, when he was an arm's length away, he grabbed at its ears and pushed its head to one side. The calf gave an angry grunt and twisted its head. Pedrinho held on with all his strength. His bare feet skidded through the red dust. He tried to twist the head again, but this time the calf gave a kick, and bucked its head so high that Pedrinho was lifted off his feet and thrown into the dust. The calf immediately bolted across the pen where it stopped and shook the lasso from its neck.

"Hopeless!" called Alberto, shaking his head. "How many times have I told you? Put one hand under its chin. Then it'll go down. Give me that lasso."

Pedrinho picked the lasso out of the dirt, walked slowly towards Alberto and handed it to him.

"Watch," said Alberto, coiling the rope into loose loops in his big brown hand.

The calf sniffed. Alberto swung the lasso above his head, once, twice then, on the third swing, let go. The loop landed clean round the calf's neck. He pulled it tight and, like Pedrinho, crossed the pen, coiling in the rope. Then he took the animal's ears in his left hand, pushed his right hand under its chin and it fell over without a sound. At once, Alberto dropped onto the calf's side, pinning it to the red earth. He slipped the lasso off, and looked across at Pedrinho. "That's how you do it," he said.

Pedrinho nodded. Alberto stood up. So did the calf. Alberto gave it a thwack on the rump and it scampered away. He coiled the lasso and tucked it in his belt. Then he spat into the dust, and walked off.

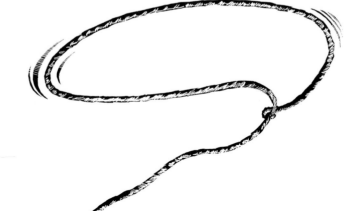

6 Plak! Plak!

Pedrinho jumped onto the fence and sat astride the top rail.

"Sometimes Alberto is angry like a dog!" he grinned.

"You're not bad with the lasso," I said.

"I'm not as good as I will be," Pedrinho replied, smiling all his small brown teeth. "Anyway, are we going to meet my friends?"

"Yes," I nodded.

"Good!" said Pedrinho, jumping down.

He headed off up the hot, dry track and I followed. We crossed a plank bridge over a slow-moving stream, and in the distance I could see the row of houses where the cowboys lived. I thought that was where we were heading, but Pedrinho suddenly ducked through a gap in the fence along the track. In front of us was a field of long grass, with a tall metal barn at one end.

"Let's go!" Pedrinho called.

I hesitated.

"What's the problem?" he asked.

"Aren't there snakes in this grass?" I asked.

"Maybe," said Pedrinho, breaking into a run.
"Swish your feet like me. It scares them off."

I nodded.

"I don't like snakes," I said, jogging after him,
and making every footstep as noisy as I could.

"That's all right," grinned Pedrinho. "They
don't like you!"

We ran up the field, away from the barn and
towards a line of trees.

"What about jaguars?" I called. "Aren't there
jaguars in the trees?"

"Hardly any now."

"How do you know?"

"Because you see scratch marks
in the bark if they're around. And
you hear them."

Pedrinho took a breath and
let out a throaty growl that
sounded like a wild cat.

"What's happened
to them?" I called.

"People shot them."

"Who?" I asked.

Pedrinho shrugged.

"Sometimes poachers."

"Was something going on last night?" I asked. "I heard people talking about guns."

"Don't know," said Pedrinho. "Sometimes Alberto goes out in the night with the cowboys and they take their guns."

"Why?"

Pedrinho ducked into some trees.

"He never tells me," he tutted.

Under our feet was a crackling carpet of dry palm branches, and above us thin trunks curved up towards the sun. Pedrinho darted softly between them as if following some invisible path. He pointed a warning finger at a tree that had long black spines up its sides.

Then, a bit further on, he stopped and nodded up. In the branches above us was an enormous bird sitting on a tattered nest of sticks.

As I peered up, its huge hollow beak went, "PLAK! PLAK!"

"It's called a 'tuiuiu'," whispered Pedrinho, slapping mosquitoes off his ankles. "It nests here every year."

I tried to say the name, but it was difficult. Whenever I said it Pedrinho screwed up his face and shook his head. Then we both started laughing. The bird heard us and flapped off into the sky, sending little specs of dust into the sunbeams around us.

We came out of the woods onto a stretch of muddy grass dotted with bushes.

"How far away do these friends live?" I asked.

"The river's just there," said Pedrinho pointing ahead. "My friends are on the other side of it."

We reached the riverbank. Pedrinho pulled off his T-shirt and started to wade out into the brown water.

"Wait!" I called out. "Where are you going?"

"Just there," said Pedrinho, pointing at a clump of trees on the other side.

I had never seen such dark, slow-moving water. There was no telling what was swimming about in it.

"Isn't there a bridge?" I asked.

Pedrinho grinned and shook his head.

"We cross here."

"But there might be piranhas."

"Yes," he said, walking on as

calmly as if he was on a zebra crossing.

I thought he must be winding me up. If there were piranha fish in the river he wouldn't be wading across it. But I still didn't feel like following. As he reached the middle of the river, the water rose so high he had to hold his T-shirt above his head.

"I might go back to the farm," I called. "Mum and Luis will be worried."

"You can't go!" he said, without looking round. "My friends are just over there!"

So I pulled off my shirt and trainers and followed.

7 Pedrinho's Secret

The water was cool. Black mud squeezed through my toes and, as I peered down, something gave a little splash near the middle of the river. I was thinking about Mum's film. Red water and bones. But I walked on, and was soon up to my stomach in the dark water. The mud was so thick that I sank to my shins with every step.

Pedrinho was already shaking water off his back under the trees on the other bank. I held my clothes above my head as the soupy water rose up to my shoulders. Something was brushing against the backs of my knees.

"Are there really piranha fish in here?" I asked.

"Lots," said Pedrinho, with a look on his face that told me he wasn't winding me up. I wrinkled up my face and sloshed out the far side of the

river, looking down at the backs of my legs.
Pedrinho was shaking with laughter.

"Don't worry, Mr English!" he grinned, sitting
down. "Piranhas only eat people on TV. If they
are trapped in still water then they bite, but not in
a river like this. They just eat fish and birds that
fall in the water – that sort of thing."

A gust of wind stirred the leaves above us. The
sun was warm and my skin glowed after the cold
water.

"Where is England?" asked Pedrinho.

"I don't know which direction it is from here,"
I told him.

"But it's one of those big countries over there,"
said Pedrinho, pointing a finger up the river.

"It's not nearly as big as Brazil."

"No?" said Pedrinho. "But you have
helicopters and satellite TV?"

"Yes," I said, and Pedrinho nodded as though
that was all he needed to know. Then he got up
and started walking away. I pulled on my trainers
and ducked after him. There was no path. We
wound between some palm trees, along the curve
of the river. And ahead of us
was a huge thicket of

trees and undergrowth. I couldn't see how we were going to get through, but Pedrinho reached down, pulled back some brown palm branches, and behind them was an opening. He ducked in and beckoned for me to follow. I crouched down and found myself in a sort of tunnel through the bushes.

The way had been carefully cut, and the ground was worn. Leaves and stems curved above us so we had to keep our heads low. The only sound was the little high-pitched calls of crickets from either side. Then, suddenly, the tunnel opened into a clearing.

To the right was thick greenery. But to the left a beach of pale sand sloped gently to the river.

And at one end of the clearing, just out of sight from the river, was a campfire with a cooking pot hanging from a metal frame. There were upturned wooden boxes to sit on, a low table made out of green palm branches, and cups and knives dangling from nails on the side of a tree.

"Wow!" I said, walking out across the sand. "A hideout."

"Yes," said Pedrinho, smiling his brown teeth. "No one knows about it. It's my biggest secret."

Then he nodded behind me and said, "And there's one of my friends."

"EHHHH!" I said, stumbling backwards.

There was an alligator with bright eyes lying in the shade, right behind me. Its mouth opened slightly as I backed off, and its long, serrated tail gave a flick.

"It might attack," I whispered.

"It's all right," smiled Pedrinho walking towards the alligator. "This one hardly ever bites."

I backed off still further, but Pedrinho walked right up to the alligator. Inside its mouth I could see sixty or seventy crooked teeth. Pedrinho looked it in the eye. Then he squatted down and patted the sand. The alligator stared straight ahead. Pedrinho carefully stretched out a hand and gave the top of its head a rub.

"You're my friend, aren't you?" he nodded.

8 Morena

I bit my teeth together as Pedrinho ran his hands along the top of the alligator's head, squeezing the bumpy, brown skin.

"Three of them live round here," he said, still looking into the alligator's eyes. "I've known them for years. This one is Morena. There's another called Preto. He's younger than Morena, but about the same size. And there's Amarela. She's a yellow-belly. She's the biggest. She's the one I know best."

I took a step closer. Morena blinked. Pedrinho edged round a little. Then he stepped over the alligator and sat down on the flat part of her back, as if she was a horse. I couldn't believe my eyes. But he reached down both his hands and started squeezing her knobbly legs. Birds whistled somewhere off in the trees. Morena closed her hooded eyes and rested her chin in the sand like a pleased cat. Pedrinho carried on massaging her legs for a few minutes, wrinkling up his face as if to say 'she loves this'. Then he got off the alligator's back and knelt in the pale sand beside her.

"You can touch her if you want," he said. "She's in a good mood."

"Are you sure she really doesn't bite?" I asked.

"If you tread on her she'd probably bite your foot off," he said, reaching out his hand and rubbing the thick, dark skin along her back. "But if you touch her like this she likes it."

I stepped slowly towards the two of them. Morena's eyes opened wide. They were yellow and fierce. She was staring straight at me and I froze where I was. At that moment, Morena thumped her legs into the sand, shot forward and went gliding off down the sand towards the water.

"If you're nervous, she's nervous," said Pedrinho, getting up and walking towards the campfire. There were red butterflies swooping about above his head. He reached into one of the wooden boxes, pulled out a hammock and strung it between two trees.

"What's the most dangerous animal in England?" he asked.

"I don't know," I said, thinking for a while. "Maybe a bull."

"A bull?" said Pedrinho. "What can a bull do?"

"It can chase you," I said.

"Only if you're stupid!" laughed Pedrinho and,

from somewhere up above us came a great raucous cackle, as if a parrot in the trees was laughing as well. Pedrinho took a lump of bread from his pocket. Then he dipped it in the water and started to soften it between his fingers. Morena stared coldly at us from the edge of the river. I could see the nostrils at the tip of her nose opening and closing as she breathed. Pedrinho raised his chin and looked across the river.

"There's Preto," he said, pointing at a shadowy stretch of water downstream. "See?"

I could see a piece of wood floating in the water but nothing else. Then the piece of wood blinked, and I realised it was a nose and two eyes. The rest of the alligator was under the water.

"Amarela sleeps there somewhere," Pedrinho added, pointing up the river. "I can't see her, but she usually comes by to say hello."

He gave the bread a last squeeze, then came back up the beach and took a stick that was propped against a tree. It was a fishing rod, with a short line and a tiny hook. He pinched a dot of bread onto the hook, flicked it into the water and, almost straight away, pulled out a small, round fish.

"Is that a piranha?" I asked.

Pedrinho looked round at me and pulled a face. "Don't they teach you anything at school?" he said. "That's a *lambari*."

9 See ... Lou ... Ya-ter ...

The *lambari* flapped between Pedrinho's fingertips as he unhooked it. Morena padded back towards us and her mouth flew open as Pedrinho tossed the *lambari* at her. Morena snapped her teeth, but too late. The fish was already wriggling on the sand. Morena tried to turn her head on its side to catch it, but the fish flicked away and all she got was a mouthful of sand.

"She has a very small brain!" grinned Pedrinho. Then he reached down and picked up the fish.

There was a hiss from behind us. I turned round. It was Preto padding out of the river. Water dripped from his throat as he lumbered up the beach. He was blacker than Morena, and a fraction bigger. I backed away again. Pedrinho ignored Preto and shook the sand off the fish. Morena arched her neck and snapped her mouth up at his hand.

Pedrinho tossed the *lambari* behind him to Preto, who caught it and swallowed it in one.

Morena snapped her mouth six inches away from Pedrinho's ankle. "Uh-uh!" he tutted, holding out the fishing rod and giving her a sharp rap on the top of her head. "You were impatient! So you lost your fish!"

Morena blinked sheepishly, dropped her head and took two small steps back.

Pedrinho put another pinch of bread on his hook and flicked it back into the river.

"There's another fishing rod by the tree if you want, Mr English," he said. I walked back up the beach and found the rod. By the time I got back, Pedrinho had already caught another *lambari* and was holding it out for Morena. This time she gulped it straight down.

The little fish were easy to catch. Soon I was pulling them out of the water and chucking them to the alligators myself. We fed Morena and Preto until they lost interest. Preto swam away and Morena lay in the sand staring straight ahead.

Pedrinho said he was going to make coffee. He put water in the cooking pot and lit a fire underneath it. I felt worn out and lay in the hammock for a while. When Pedrinho handed me a cup I sat up. The coffee was strong and sweet.

"Has the other alligator turned up?" I asked.

"Amarela?" said Pedrinho. "I don't know where she is."

"She's bigger than the others?"

"Much bigger ... and more bad-tempered," laughed Pedrinho. "And she likes it when I tickle her!"

I looked at my watch.

"I need to go back," I said.

"All right," Pedrinho nodded, finishing his coffee.

He took the cups down to rinse in the river,

then folded the hammock away. I propped the fishing rods back against the tree, took one last look at Morena lying in the sand and said, in English, "*SEE YOU LATER ALLIGATOR!*"

Pedrinho gave me a funny look, so I explained what 'see you later alligator' means.

"*SEE ... LOU ... YA-TER ... ALLI-GAT-OH,*" said Pedrinho, and ducked back into the tunnel through the bushes.

When we came out the other side he carefully put back the palm branches to hide the tunnel. We walked on to where we had crossed the river. But Pedrinho kept going. He had spotted something further along. All I could see was a couple of green birds flapping quietly away, but Pedrinho jumped down onto some sand and stopped.

"What is it?" I asked.

"Someone's been here," he called.

I jumped after him and, as I walked across the sand, I could make out footprints.

"Last night," said Pedrinho, squatting down.

"There were three people, maybe more. They came out of those bushes and went running off that way."

He pointed in the opposite direction we had come from. Then he stood up and shook his head.

"They were shooting."
He picked up an
empty, red shotgun
cartridge. "Here's
another," I said, spotting a
second cartridge case
further along the beach.
"Who was it?" I asked.
"Poachers," said Pedrinho.
"They sell animal skins. Someone is
killing a lot of animals round here."

He stood up and tutted.

"Perhaps they shot Amarela."

He chucked the cartridge case back onto the
sand and started to follow the footprints into the
trees. As soon as he pushed past the first
branches, there was a snapping sound from up
ahead. I stepped back. Pedrinho lowered his
head, peered through the leaves and there was an
angry outburst of calls. Then four or five huge,
black birds flapped out.

"Vultures," said Pedrinho, pushing into the
bushes.

I followed and Pedrinho stopped.

"Look," he said, nodding to his left.

I couldn't see anything.

"On the tree," he said softly.

10 The Anaconda

Looking through the leaves I saw something long hanging from the tree. It was white, like the backbone of a huge fish.

"What's that?" I whispered.

"An anaconda," said Pedrinho, ducking under a branch towards the tree. "The poachers skinned it here."

As we got closer, flies buzzed in the air and my nose filled with a smell like rotten fish.

The snake must have been three metres long. Its tail was tied tightly to a branch with a piece of wire. The rest was slumped on the ground in two fat coils. And its mouth hung loosely from its head.

"See what they did?" said Pedrinho. "Killed it. Then peeled its skin off. It's worth money."

"It's huge," I whispered.

Pedrinho shrugged and picked up the snake's pale head. "This one's only a baby," he shrugged.

"They broke its head. With a stick."

"With a stick?" I said.

Pedrinho tutted again. "It was very easy to kill. There's a bird or something in its stomach." He pointed to a bulge halfway along the snake. "The snake had just eaten. So it was sleepy."

He turned away. "Let's go," he said. "It stinks worse than the hen house."

We waded across the river again and wove our way back through the trees. I picked up a stick to push back the branches.

"You won't tell anyone where we went, will you?" said Pedrinho.

"Perhaps I'd better tell Luis about the dead snake," I said.

Pedrinho turned round and shook his head. "Alberto doesn't like me coming down here. He says it disturbs the animals. If he finds out about the hideout he'll get angry."

"Well," I said, "if my mum finds out where I've been she's not going to be very happy either!"

Pedrinho raised his eyebrows. "And if no one finds out we can come back tomorrow!"

"I'm going to have to tell Mum and Luis something," I said.

Pedrinho gave a shrug as we stepped out of the trees into the field near the barn. "Just say we met some friends of mine and went fishing. It's the truth. Sometimes I go and play football with some boys who live on the farm. Though I'd rather go to the hideout. They're rubbish at football. They play like English players."

I threw my stick at Pedrinho and he ran away laughing.

"We won the World Cup in 1966!" I shouted.

"We won the World Cup in 1958 ... in 1962 ... in 1970 ... in 1994 and in 2002!" he shouted, racing off across the grass.

Back at the farmhouse I had a shower and put on some long trousers. It was good to be indoors again. My legs were tired and my face felt warm. But the smell of the dead snake seemed to stay in my nose.

I went out onto the balcony looking for Mum and Luis. They weren't around, but I saw Alberto down in the yard. He was standing talking to the cowboy we'd seen – Toucan. I couldn't hear everything they were saying. It was something about a new tractor Alberto was trying to get Luis to buy. I peered through the railing at the thick belt Alberto was wearing. The shotgun cartridges in it were red. Just like the ones down by the river.

We all went to bed early. The sheets on my bed felt cool as I fell asleep listening to the sounds of the animals in the warm air. Now that I'd been into the swamp their noises sounded different.

Something woke me: a popping sound, off in the distance. Guns perhaps. I looked at my watch. It was just after four. I sat up in bed and listened. Everything was quiet apart from the crickets outside. I got up, went to the window and gently pushed at the shutters. They swung open and cool air washed into the room.

Outside the night was clear and everything was still. I stood there until mosquitoes began to buzz round my face. I decided to go back to bed. But then I saw it – a pinprick of light between the trees. I leaned forward on the windowsill. The light was bobbing along as though someone was walking through the trees with a torch. I watched it come out into the field of long grass. For a moment I thought I could make out a figure. Whoever it was walked slowly towards the big barn. Then they went inside and turned a light on. There seemed to be two men and they were carrying something. Then they shut the barn door and disappeared back into the trees. I went to get Luis.

11 Probably Nothing

"Luis!" I whispered, knocking on the bedroom door. There was silence. I tapped again and a light came on.

"Ant?" came Luis' voice.

"You've got to wake up, Luis," I whispered through the door. "There's something going on."

Moments later the door opened and Luis appeared, dressed in a T-shirt and shorts. "What's going on?" he blinked.

"Did you hear shooting?"

He shook his head.

"I think someone was firing a gun in the swamp. Then I saw two men putting something in the barn."

"Sounds like a dream to me," said Luis.

"It's not," I told him.

"Is Alberto awake?" he asked.

"I don't know."

Luis nodded and said, "We'll go and find him."

"What's going on?" came Mum's voice from inside the room.

"Probably nothing," whispered Luis. "We'll be back in a moment."

We went out into the yard. Everything was cool and silver. Luis glanced underneath the veranda.

"The car's not there," he whispered. "So Alberto's up and about."

"I think it was him shooting," I said.

"Why on earth would he be shooting at this time?" replied Luis. "Where did you say you saw these people?"

"Up at the barn," I said. "Look, the light's still on."

"Well, we'll see who it is then," said Luis, and he headed up the track.

As we got nearer the barn he said, "Listen. Let's go slowly and quietly. It's probably nothing to be worried about. But remember there are no policemen just around the corner if there's trouble out here."

I nodded. Luis stared into the trees, then over at the barn.

"Where did you see them go?" he asked in a hushed voice.

"Into the trees," I said. "Just up there."

And as I pointed, there was a cracking sound from the trees.

"Get down," whispered Luis. "Someone's coming. I want to see who it is."

The two of us dropped into the grass and listened for footsteps. For a moment everything was still. The air smelled of leaves. A cricket clicked somewhere in front of us. Then I heard footsteps. They were coming towards us. A voice hissed, as though one man was telling another to hurry up. Then a torch winked. Luis and I pressed ourselves flat to the ground and I could glimpse one of the men through the grass. He was carrying a large, dark bundle and pointing the torch directly ahead. I couldn't see his face. As he turned towards the barn, the torch threw a great ark of light across the field. It swept right over the place we were lying. For a moment the grass lit up, green and bright, and I pressed my cheek into the earth so hard it hurt. I heard Luis stir slightly and looked round. He held up a finger as if to say 'Don't make a single sound.'

A second man had appeared now. He was also carrying something heavy, and it hid his head from us. Neither of them spoke as they approached the barn. You could just hear their legs swishing through the grass. The second man put his bundle down. It was Alberto. I knew at once. He had his shotgun over his left shoulder, his lasso in his belt and his hat on his head.

"That's Alberto," I whispered.

Luis gave a nod as the two men disappeared into the barn.

"What shall we do?"

"Nothing yet," said Luis. "I want to find out what they're putting in there."

I tried to shift round to get a better view inside the barn and, as I did, my shoe scraped noisily at the earth. Alberto came out of the barn. He put a hand up to the strap of his shotgun and seemed to be listening. As far as I could tell, he was looking straight at us. Luis held up his finger again. Then the other man came out. Now I could see who it was – Toucan. He also had a gun over one shoulder. Alberto looked around again. He said something very softly, turned round and shut the barn door. Then the two of them disappeared back into the trees.

When their torch was completely out of sight I looked across at Luis.

"Come on. Quickly," he said. "They've left the light on so they're obviously coming back."

I followed him towards the door of the barn. Luis pushed at it, but it had two iron locks through heavy bolts.

"What about up there?" I said. Directly above the door, light was coming out through a kind of air vent.

Luis looked doubtful.

"If you lift me I can get up," I said.

"All right," Luis nodded. "Just look quickly to see what's inside. You can use me like a ladder."

He steadied himself with his feet slightly apart. Then he lifted me so I was sitting on his shoulders.

"Can you stand up?" he asked.

Slowly I got to my feet. But I was still below the vent.

"Forget it! It's too high," said Luis. "They might be coming back."

But, by stretching up I could reach a bar that was bolted just below the vent. "Hold on," I said, and grabbed the bar with both hands. Then I pulled myself up.

"That's it!" whispered Luis. "Can you see anything?"

"Not yet," I said, gripping with all my strength and pulling myself further, until my head rose into the beam of light

12 Call the Police!

I recognised the smell straight away. It was like the dead snake.

"What's in there?" hissed Luis.

"Animal skins," I said. "Lots of them, all bundled up."

"All right," said Luis. "That's all I need to know. Come back down."

I gripped hold of the bar and let myself back down onto his shoulders. We wobbled for a moment. Then Luis reached up his hands, steadied my hips and helped me down.

"We'll wait for them to come back," said Luis. "It looks as though this Alberto of ours is not everything he pretends to be."

It wasn't long before we saw the torch again. And as it neared the edge of the trees Luis called out, "Alberto! What do you think you're doing?"

The torch immediately clicked off.

"Mr Luis?" called Alberto's deep voice. "That you?"

"It is. And I want to know what you're doing."

Alberto came out of the trees with Toucan behind him. They were carrying more skins. Alberto didn't say anything. He just walked up to the barn and threw the skins onto the ground. They splayed out at different angles. Some looked like alligator skins, some looked like snake skins, some were an orange colour and I guessed they were jaguar skins.

"They are not mine," said Alberto, touching a finger to his moustache.

"Then who do they belong to?" snapped Luis.

"They belong to the animals they were taken from," said Alberto, poking at the skins with the toe of an old dry boot.

"It was a gang of poachers that shot them," said Toucan, still holding the bundle of skins on his shoulder. "They were here last night but we scared them off. Then we heard their boat again tonight …"

"They were using our river to try to get into Bolivia to sell these skins," interrupted Alberto.

"I shouted at them, told them that it was private land and they shot at us."

"They shot at you?" I said.

Alberto nodded.

"You're all right though?" asked Luis.

Alberto nodded.

"We shoot better than them," grinned Toucan.

"You shot back?" asked Luis.

"We shot back," nodded Alberto. "And we shot better."

"We hit the engine of the boat," said Toucan. "It blew. Then they had to run for it."

"And these skins are what they had on board," said Alberto. He unlocked the barn and pulled open the big metal door.

Luis stepped inside and stood with his hands on his hips, staring at the skins piled up against the walls. Some were wrinkled and pale, others dark and stiff.

"My grandfather would turn in his grave if he knew about this," he muttered.

Toucan ran his brown fingers down one of the stacks of skins. "Alligators," he said. "Jaguars, foxes, even otters ... look ..."

"Someone has to stop them," said Alberto. "They think they can shoot whatever they like."

"Why didn't you tell me this was going on?"

said Luis, angrily holding up his hands.

"The way they ran off last night I didn't think they would be back," said Alberto, raising his heavy eyebrows, "and I didn't want to worry you and your wife and the boy here. These are dangerous men. They're only interested in money. They don't like anyone trying to stop them. A man who lives on another farm reported them a few years back and, when they found out, they cut off one of his hands."

"What if they do something to us?" I asked.

Alberto gave a little tut and shook his head. "I can look after us," he said, patting his shotgun. "But we've got to get these skins away from here quickly. They won't come during the day, but if the skins are still here tomorrow night they'll try to get them back."

"We've got to call the police," said Luis.

Alberto nodded. "But don't go to the local police. They are crooks themselves."

"Leave it to me," said Luis. "My cousin's a chief inspector in the state capital. I'll get him to send someone down to pick this stuff up."

As we walked back I felt shaky. I think Luis noticed because he put a hand on my shoulder as we walked along. Then he said, "Wherever you go you will meet bad people. But wherever you go you will meet good people."

13 I'm Going Back to See

My room with its old furniture and blue
shutters felt strangely small when we got
back. I went to sleep, and it was after ten
when I woke again. I could hear voices from
the kitchen.

Mum and Luis were sitting in there and Lúcia
was cutting up tomatoes and onions. Luis was
telling them all about what had happened in the
night. He said he'd spoken to his cousin by radio,
and the state police would be coming, but it
would take them some time to make the long
journey. Apparently, they knew there was a gang
of poachers working in the area.

Outside it was a little cooler and, for the first
time since arriving, there were clouds in the sky.
Pedrinho was up one end of the yard. There was a
big pile of logs beside him and he was splitting
them with an axe.

"All right, Mr English?" he grinned, wiping sweat from his neck.

"All right," I said. "Can I help?"

He shook his head and carried on chopping.

"Did you hear what happened in the night?" I asked.

He nodded. "I told you. It was poachers. They've been killing many animals." He swung his axe with an angry thud. Pieces of split wood bounced off into the dust. Then he added, "Maybe they shot Amarela. I'm going back to see when I've finished this."

He bent over and picked another log from the pile.

"Can I come too?" I asked.

"Of course," he said.

For a while Pedrinho carried on splitting the logs and neither of us said anything. Then he rested the axe on his shoulder and paused to catch his breath. I looked at his dusty bare feet and said, "Is there really an insect round here that burrows into your foot and lays eggs?"

"Yes," said Pedrinho.

"Has one ever burrowed into your foot?" I asked.

Pedrinho nodded. "We call it *bicho de pé*. You have to get it out by burning it."

I turned down my
mouth.

"Don't worry," he
shrugged. "It
doesn't hurt
much."

Then he looked up at the sky and said, "It's
going to rain. But not until later."

When he'd finished, we headed up the dirt track
and jogged off into the long grass. Above us two
vultures turned lazily in the sky. Pedrinho wanted
to see what was in the barn, but the door was still
locked, so we headed for the river.

It felt good to duck into the trees again. As we
walked through them, Pedrinho bent down and
picked up a couple of small yellow things like
nuts. He gave me one, bit the top off another,
peeled back the yellow skin, and stuck it in his
mouth. I did the same. Under the skin was a pale
stone. I put it in my mouth. It was like an oily
toffee.

"Palm nut," said Pedrinho. "Good for you."

We walked through the quiet shadows with the
palm nuts bulging in our cheeks. Then, near the
edge of the trees, Pedrinho held up his hand.

"Shhh," he said, peering out across the stretch
of grass that led down to the river. Then he

pointed a finger to his right. Through the leaves I could see a group of dark animals biting at the grass. They looked like pigs, but with square-ish faces. We watched them for a minute. Then Pedrinho took a couple of steps forward. The animals heard him and bolted off, making funny little grunting sounds. Pedrinho grinned as they cantered across the muddy grass and sploshed straight into the river.

"What are they ... pigs?" I asked.

"No!" tutted Pedrinho. "They're capybaras. Don't you have capybaras in England?"

I shook my head. Pedrinho turned down his mouth as if to say, "Well what do you have in England then?"

At the riverbank we stripped off and waded across. This time I didn't think twice about it, and soon we were both dripping on the far bank. I helped Pedrinho pull away the long palm branches. Then we ducked into the undergrowth.

When I came out of the tunnel Pedrinho was already walking away down the beach. Preto was down near the water. I recognised him by his dark tail. In the shallows a row of four or five birds with long legs stood side by side, like important old men. As I was looking at them Pedrinho spotted something and started walking quickly to the far end of the beach. The birds with long legs flapped off over the trees.

"Is it Amarela?" I called, trudging through the sand after him.

Pedrinho didn't reply. He had reached the shadowy place where the undergrowth reached right down to the edge of the river. There he stepped carefully out into the dark, shallow water and reached down with his hand. I couldn't see what was in the water. Then I saw a pale shape, rocking slowly from side to side. As I got closer I realised it was an alligator, motionless in the water, rolled over onto its back with its feet pointing up at the sun.

"Is it Amarela?" I repeated.

"It's Morena," said Pedrinho, without turning round. "Look."

14 Real Fishing

I stood beside Pedrinho as he reached down and turned the big, bobbing body round. Fish darted away as the water stirred. Water spilt from between her teeth. The stumpy legs he had been massaging the day before stuck out stiffly and, when she was the right way up, I recognised her bumpy brown snout. But her eyes were closed.

"She's dead," I said.

Pedrinho nodded, squatted down and ran a hand along the top of her leathery head.

"They shot her," he said.

Preto shifted behind us and his skin squeaked like new shoes. Pedrinho pulled a lump of bread from his pocket and tossed it to me.

"Make some bait to catch *lambari*," he said. "I'm going to take you up the river to a special place I know. Whenever I go fishing there Amarela comes."

I dipped the bread in the water and started to

squeeze it into dough. Preto slowly closed his eyes.

Pedrinho went to get the fishing rods and we started fishing for *lambari*. As soon as I pulled out the first one Preto's hooded eyes opened and he gave a flick of his knobbly tail, but Pedrinho said not to give him the fish. Instead he put a wooden box in the water and we dropped the *lambari* inside that.

When we had enough, Pedrinho went up to the campfire and came back with a big knife in a leather sheath, two tins and a brown sack. He tipped the small fish out of the box into the sack.

"You bring this," he said, handing it to me.

We crawled back through the tunnel, then walked along the riverbank further than we had the day before. Soon we were in the shadows of tall trees. It was a patch of forest, darker and cooler than the one near the farm. The trees reached high above us and their trunks were damp.

Some way into the forest, Pedrinho ducked under some creepers and back towards the river. Ahead I could see a little earthy ledge that jutted out on a curve in the river. The water looked deeper and darker than it did down the river. Trees leaned right out over the water and their branches blocked most of the sky. Pedrinho led the way up onto the ledge and sat down. I crouched beside him as he looked up the river. Then he handed me one of the tins he was carrying. It had a thick fishing line coiled round it and a big silver hook at the end of each line.

"We're going to do some real fishing," he said.

He chopped a *lambari* into three pieces. Then he took a piece and pushed it onto one of the big hooks.

"You will catch piranhas!" he said, nodding at the far side of the river. He uncoiled a good length of line from the tin, swung the bait round his head, just like the lasso, then let it fly. It landed with a splash on the other side of the river.

I unravelled my line and baited the hook in the same way. Then I swung it round my head, and sent it into the air as hard as I could. But instead of splashing on the other side of the river, it landed right in front of me. I looked down and realised why. I was standing on the line.

Before I even had time to wind in my line and try again, Pedrinho tugged on his and started pulling it in. Something dark wriggled through the weed below us as Pedrinho coiled the line in. Then a fat fish came flicking out of the water on the end of his line. It was about twice the size of my hand. Its stomach was a muddy colour. The fins along its back were almost red. Its big, blunt lower jaw was open and, inside, were two lines of vicious teeth

"Piranha?" I asked

"Piranha," nodded Pedrinho.

He ran his thumb and forefinger softly up the fish's sides and into the gills behind its head. From somewhere inside came an angry little sound. It flicked once, but Pedrinho had a safe grip on it, and pulled the hook from the corner of its mouth. He held it out for me to see. Its teeth were sharp triangles that fitted together perfectly.

"Piranha," he repeated, looking out across the river, with the fish still between his fingers. He stood there, gazing for a time. Then he took a deep breath and said, "I've lost my friend."

"Amarela?" I said.

"She loves piranhas. She always comes when I fish here. I always feed her …"

He rubbed his forehead with his knuckles, then bent down and dropped the piranha into the sack.

"Perhaps she's somewhere up the river," I said.

"They killed her," said Pedrinho, without looking at me.

15 Lashing Tail

We carried on fishing in silence. The deep water was full of piranhas. The moment my bait hit the water I could feel them biting. But whenever I pulled in my line there was just a bony scrap of bait left on the hook.

"When they bite," said Pedrinho, "tug at the line. Then pull it in."

I nodded and watched as he reeled in another piranha. Then I tossed my line out across the river again. Something bit. I tugged. It felt heavy. I pulled in the line, peering into the murky water and smiled as a piranha appeared, darting from side to side. Pedrinho watched as I pulled the fish out of the water.

"You caught it, Mr English," he said. "Now you have to get it off the hook without it catching you!"

I dangled the fish on the line in

front of me. Its eyes stared at the sky and its stubby lower jaw clicked shut. Then I carefully ran the forefinger and thumb of my left hand up its sides and into its gills like Pedrinho had. The fish flicked but I kept my grip on it. Its mouth opened, showing its razor teeth.

"With your fingers like that, its mouth will stay open," said Pedrinho moving closer.

"Yes?"

"Yes."

I reached down and pulled out the hook. All my attention was focused on the tough little fish. But, at that moment, there was a dark stirring in the water in front of us. As I looked down, the piranha flicked fiercely and I had to tighten my grip to keep hold of it. At the same time the burnt colours of a huge head exploded out of the water.

"Amarela!" said Pedrinho. "She's alive!"

The alligator in front of us was enormous – twice the length of the others we had seen. It looked like some kind of dinosaur rearing out of the river with gaping jaws. I froze as an angry growl came from deep inside her throat and she came sploshing towards us on powerful webbed feet. Without hesitating Pedrinho put down his line and stepped into the shallow water in front of her. Amarela growled even more ferociously. Pedrinho flicked a bit of water at her head with his foot.

"All right, Amarela?" he asked, squatting down. "Where have you been?"

The alligator let out a hiss like a great rush of escaping steam and ducked her head slightly under the water. Pedrinho reached out a hand and wiggled his fingers. The animal's head rose out of the water and he moved his hand closer. Amarela shifted her baggy neck and Pedrinho ran his hand over the leathery bumps of her head. As he did, his neck stiffened and he said, "They did try to shoot her. Look."

He pointed to a white cut through the dark skin just behind Amarela's eyes.

Amarela hissed, but only softly. He rubbed the flat of her snout and she lifted her head towards the fish in my hand. Pedrinho smiled up. "You'd better give her that piranha before she helps herself!"

Amarela narrowed her eyes. The piranha flicked sharply between my fingers. Amarela's gums glistened as she raised her head towards my hand. I took a step forward then tossed down the piranha.

The alligator snatched it out of the air. There was one big crunch as her jaw snapped shut. Then she narrowed her eyes and swallowed. Pedrinho laughed and clapped. Amarela hissed and backed away.

We carried on fishing and most of what we caught we fed to Amarela. When she'd had enough, we put the fish in the sack. Pedrinho said he'd take them back for Lúcia. He was back to his old self, chattering away. Amarela floated in the shadows beside us and she almost looked as though she was grinning at the silly jokes Pedrinho and I kept making.

After a while it began to cloud right over and Pedrinho asked if I wanted to go back.

"Let's stay a bit," I said. "We're leaving tomorrow. After that I won't be able to come here."

"All right," said Pedrinho, picking up the knife, the sack of piranhas and the tins. "Come and see what's over here."

He looked down at Amarela who was sleeping in the shallows.

"See you later alligator!" I said, and Pedrinho grinned.

16 Weren't You Scared?

We walked a little way round the river's curve and came to a beach. At one end an old tree bent over the river. Pedrinho dropped what he was carrying in the sand and ran towards the tree. It had one thick branch sticking out, three or four metres above the water, and vines hugging its trunk. He scrabbled up the vines. I kicked off my trainers and followed. It was easy to climb, and the high branch was so thick you could walk along it.

"Cool, eh?" said Pedrinho, as we stood perched above the middle river. "And so's the water!"

"You're not going to jump, are you?" I asked.

Pedrinho shook his head. "You are! You smell like a bushpig! You need a bath!"

Before I could react he gave me a shove. I braced myself as best I could, but Pedrinho had a better foothold than I did. For a moment we were locked together. Then I tumbled, spinning down, and plunged into the darkness of the river. I burst back up through the surface ready to swear at Pedrinho. But he had already jumped and landed with a great splash beside me.

"You nut head!" I shouted, swimming back to the foot of the tree.

"You tortoise!" he shouted, getting to the bank before me and clambering up the vines again. I wasn't far behind and almost caught his ankle as he pulled himself up onto the branch. He let out a laugh and scrambled to the end. I raced after and he stood waiting for me. Birds squawked. I ran with my head down and would have sent him flying, but he waited until I was a whisker away then jumped with a whoop. I didn't even stop. I just kept running into the air and dropped down into the black river.

I don't know how many times we jumped. Sometimes I got pushed off. Sometimes he did. Lots of times one of us lost our balance but gripped onto the other, so we went spinning into the water together. It was only when we heard rumblings of thunder in the distance that we decided to head back.

Everything was quiet at the farmhouse. There was no sign of Alberto's pick-up and Pedrinho said he had to stack the chopped wood before it started raining. I put down the sack of piranhas we'd brought back for Lúcia, and walked across to give him a hand.

As I did, I heard the sound of a car. I thought it must be Alberto. But it wasn't. It was a black pick-up bouncing towards us with a trail of red dust behind it. As it drew closer I saw there were two policemen inside. Both wore beige baseball caps pulled low over their eyes. The one driving had a friendly, round face and was chewing gum. He looked about the same age as Luis, or a little older.

"Lads," he said, winding down the window. "Is this where some animal skins have been found?"

"In the barn," I said. The second policeman stared at me from the passenger seat. He was taller than the other, with a thin face.

"Is it locked?"

I nodded.

"Alberto's got the keys."

The round-faced policeman got out of the car and looked about the yard with his quick eyes. His legs were short and his shoulders heavy. There was a silver pistol in a holster hanging from his belt and a torch tucked in the other side.

"Is Alberto the owner of this farm?" he asked.

"He's the farm manager," I said. "The owner's my stepfather, Luis."

The thin policeman got out of the car, and the round-faced one held out a hand. "Where are you from?" he asked.

"England," I said, shaking his hand.

"A real-life Englishman in the Pantanal," he smiled, not letting go of my hand. "I know about England. David Beckham. Michael Owen. Arsenal!"

Across the yard the front door opened and Luis and Mum came down the steps.

"Mr Luis?" said the round-faced policeman. "I'm Sergeant Batista and this is my colleague, Military Policeman Oliveira."

"We were hoping you'd come before nightfall," said Luis, shaking hands.

"Do you live here?" asked Sergeant Batista.

"My family owns the land," said Luis.

"We received reports of shooting," said Batista. His hands rested comfortably on his stomach as he talked, but his eyes shifted restlessly. Luis explained what had happened.

"I want you to do everything to catch these people," he told the policeman. "Those skins are a horrific sight."

"We'll take them away with us," said Batista.

"They are up in the barn," nodded Luis. "I'll show you before it gets dark."

He told Pedrinho to run and fetch Alberto.

"You don't have keys yourself?" asked Batista, spitting his chewing gum onto the ground.

"No," said Luis.

We all walked across the yard towards the track. Thunder was rumbling nearby now. Mum asked if I'd had a good afternoon. I picked up the sack of piranhas and showed her.

"You caught those?" Luis smiled.

"About half of them."

"Can you eat piranhas?" asked Mum, wrinkling up her face.

Sergeant Batista nodded. "They make you strong!"

Then he looked at me and asked, "Weren't you scared?"

"Not really," I said.

He smiled as though he didn't believe me and added, "What about if you saw a jaguar?"

"My friend says there aren't any jaguars left round here," I shrugged.

"That's what the jaguars want you to think," winked Sergeant Batista.

Luis smiled but, as we got nearer to the barn, I had a nervous feeling, as though something was about to go wrong.

17 Alberto's Problem

There was no sign of Alberto at the barn.

"He'll be here in a moment," said Luis.

Darkness was falling and, every now and then, lightning dazzled across the sky. Oliveira had a closer look at the locks on the barn door. Batista took off his baseball cap and wiped his forehead.

Then Alberto's pick-up came bumping towards us out of the dusk.

He got out, slinging his shotgun over his shoulder and Pedrinho jumped out of the other side.

"Sorry to keep you," said Alberto, jingling his keys.

But, when he saw Oliveira, the look on his face changed.

"I've seen you before," he said.

Oliveira stared back. Batista sniffed and put

his baseball cap back on.

"I've been a policeman round here for years," nodded Oliveira. "You probably have seen me."

"I saw you last night," said Alberto.

Oliveira gave a little huff. "I …" he said, but Batista interrupted.

"I don't know where you were last night, my friend," he smiled, "but, wherever it was, Oliveira wasn't there. Now, shall we open this barn?"

"No," said Alberto, closing his fingers around the keys.

"What's your problem, Alberto?" asked Luis, angrily. "These are policemen."

Alberto nodded. "This one here is a poacher as well," he said. "I saw him on that boat last night. And this other one is probably no better. They've come to get the skins."

Sergeant Batista gave a strange laugh that seemed to stick somewhere down his throat. And something in his face had changed. His chin jutted angrily. His eyes narrowed. He looked like Amarela with her eyes on a fish. Both he and Oliveira reached for their pistols. They didn't point them at anyone, just held them in their hands. I put down the sack of fish. Mum clutched Luis' arm and I could see sweat glistening across his forehead.

Batista stared Alberto in the eyes. His lips were pulled tight across his teeth.

"I'm a policeman!" he said. "Now open that barn."

Big drops of rain were beginning to fall. Alberto shook his head. Oliveira shook his head as well. Batista nodded at Luis.

"Tell your man to give me the keys," he said, flicking his pistol in the air.

"Wait a minute," said Luis' holding out his hands. "We don't need guns."

Sergeant Batista gave Luis a steely stare. A heavier wave of rain swept across us out of the darkening sky. "Get your man to give me the key or shut your mouth," he said.

"Put away those guns!" said Mum in a shrill voice.

"We're not pointing them at anyone," said Batista. "But we will if we have to."

"And you'll shoot innocent people, just like you shoot innocent animals?" asked Alberto.

His dark eyes were fixed on the face of the short policeman. Then he turned to Oliveira. "And you!" he said. "Are you from round here?"

"Yes," said Oliveira.

Alberto nodded.

"Pantanal men are proud of this place and the

creatures that live here," he said. "You're a
disgrace to where you're from."

"Button your beak," snapped Batista, stepping
forward and swiping his hand at Alberto's head,
knocking his hat onto the ground. "And give me
the keys!"

At that Alberto reached for his shotgun.

"Do what he says," hissed Oliveira, "or you'll
get the first bullet!"

"No!" called Luis.

"Don't!" I called out.

"Throw that gun
on the ground!"
ordered Sergeant
Batista.

With the pistols pointed at him, Alberto had no choice. He shrugged the shotgun off his shoulder and tossed it with a thud onto the ground. Oliveira bent down and picked it up. Then he tossed it into a ditch beside the barn. It landed with a splash.

"Put down your guns," said Luis, calmly stepping towards the policemen. "Let's resolve this as human beings."

Batista ignored him.

"Give us the keys," he said, jabbing his pistol towards Alberto. "Or we'll cut you in half like the snake you are!"

His face was screwed up as though he'd smelled a dead dog. But Alberto stared straight back.

"You won't," he said, and as soon as the words were out of his mouth, the policeman's pistol cracked and flashed yellow light.

18 Let Them Go!

One of Alberto's arms kicked up like a rubber band.
A metallic smell filled the air. It was Oliveira who
had fired. Alberto gritted his teeth. The bullet had hit
him on the wrist.

"No!" shouted Pedrinho, and he started to run
towards Alberto. But Mum caught hold of him and
held him back.

"The keys," said Batista.

"Do what he says, Alberto!" screamed Mum.
"He's a maniac!"

"Give him the keys or you'll get yourself killed,
Alberto!" shouted Luis.

Alberto gave a little shake of his head and tossed
the keys onto the ground in front of him. I
remember the sour smell of the gunshot, the coolness
of the rain, Sergeant Batista saying "Thank you".

Then Oliveira bent down to pick up the keys. But,
at the same moment, Pedrinho dived out of Mum's

grip and grabbed the keys. Oliveira stood frozen for a moment, like a goalkeeper who has let in a goal without even seeing the ball. And in one fluent movement Pedrinho dived between his legs and ran for the trees. Mum screamed, picked up the bag of piranha fish and swung it at Batista. The policemen, with their pistols pointed at Alberto, were caught completely by surprise.

Batista lurched to his left to avoid the sack of piranha fish and then to his right to try to grab at Pedrinho. Pedrinho swerved out of harm's way, and that was when I spun round and ran with him for the trees.

"No!" screamed Mum. But it was too late to change my mind.

Pedrinho was half a stride ahead of me as we plunged into darkness. My head was a jumble of feelings: fear, anger, amazement.

"Ant!" I heard Luis shout.

Then Mum's voice was shrieking, "Let them go! They're only boys!"

But her shouting didn't make any difference because, an instant later, I heard branches snapping behind us and Sergeant Batista bellowing, "Through there! Don't let them get away!"

Rain drummed on the leaves around us. Pedrinho dodged between inky bushes and tree trunks with his fingers bunched round the keys. He moved lightly and quickly on his bare feet and I followed each twist and turn that he made.

He seemed to deliberately head for where the undergrowth was thickest and, before long, I realised why. It was easier for us to duck under the low branches than it was for the two men coming after us. I could hear them cursing and stumbling as the trees blocked and snagged their way.

"Stop!" shouted Batista. "Stop! Or you'll regret it!"

I glanced over my shoulder and could see they had lit their torches and were pushing slowly after us, like a pair of bulls in mud.

Pedrinho twisted round as well. "Let's go, Mr English!" he said, through gritted teeth. "They won't catch us now!"

He was right. With every tree we passed, their frustrated footsteps fell further behind.

"I don't understand," I panted, as we ran. "They're policeman."

"They're corrupt policemen," called back Pedrinho. "They've been helping poachers smuggle skins."

"That Batista is a scumbag," I said, breathlessly. "I wish I'd never shaken hands with him."

"I hope you counted your fingers after you did," said Pedrinho.

He pressed on, his head held high and his shoulders weaving from side to side.

"This is the way to the hideout," I said.

"That's where we've got to get to," said Pedrinho. "I know every curve of the river round there, and they don't."

He slowed to a jog for the first time. We were both panting. I looked round and could see the torches flicking between the tree trunks. The policemen weren't as far behind as I'd thought. In fact, one of the beams suddenly swept towards me and flashed across my face.

I heard Oliveira call, "There they are!"

"Come on!" said Pedrinho, zipping off again down the path. "Once they find this path they'll start catching up."

I ran as fast as I can ever remember running. Creepers snatched at my knees, twigs scratched at my arms, and I had to twist my head to stop branches springing in my face. Then, without warning, we were out into the black rain and the muddy field that led to the river. There was a stuttering sound up ahead as ten or twelve capybaras went twisting off into the grass. The rain made my hair cling to my face. My lungs felt raw. Even my teeth ached as we belted towards the river. It was like being foxes chased by dogs. All I wanted in the world was to get to the river before they came out of the trees.

19 Let Yourself Drift

Twenty metres short of the river I heard Batista's voice, "Got you!" he yelled.

I waited for the sound of a shot. Maybe they couldn't see us in the rain. Maybe they thought they'd catch us easily in the water. I'll never know. I just careered over the edge of the riverbank and plunged alongside Pedrinho into the blackness of the water.

When I bobbed up to the surface I was already out into the middle of the river. I put a hand onto Pedrinho's shoulder and whispered, "Let's swim to the hideout! If we get straight out the other side they'll see us."

Pedrinho nodded and put a finger up to his lips to show that we had to be completely silent. We kept our arms under the water and paddled down the river, with the slow current helping us. Soon we were in the dark shadows of the river's curve. Beyond it was the beach that led up to the hideout.

"What now?" I whispered.

"We've got to keep them guessing," said Pedrinho, so softly that I could barely hear him. "I'm going to try to confuse them. You stay in the water. Let yourself drift right round the curve. And you take the keys."

With that, his small, strong hand passed me the cold bunch of keys. "Watch out for the alligators," he added before he went. "They're more dangerous at night."

Pedrinho disappeared into the rain with an almost silent swish and I felt a twist of fear as I heard the policemen's footsteps. Then I saw them, Batista first, grey as a ghost in the rain.

All I could do was let myself drift. The policemen scanned the river. The beams of their torches lit up the rain and skimmed across the water towards me. The current wasn't pulling me fast enough, so I kicked under the water. Then my feet touched sand and I waded slowly towards the dark shadows of the trees at the edge of the hideout. The keys dug into the palm of my hand.

When I looked back I caught sight of Pedrinho. Instead of crossing the river, he had let himself drift back to the same bank the policemen were on. He slipped into the thick bushes to their left, so I could see him but they could not.

Then he picked up something and lobbed it across the river. It landed with a thud on the far bank.

Immediately both torch beams flew across the river. I heard Oliveira say, "There's something over there."

Batista beckoned Oliveira to follow him into the water. Pedrinho didn't move. He waited until they had waded just over half-way across. Then he made a low growling sound that carried through the rain, right the way across the river.

Immediately the torches stopped moving.

"What was that?" Batista asked.

"That was a jaguar," came Oliveira's voice.

"Don't be ridiculous," said Batista. "It's one of the boys. He's back there."

He tried to turn, but the mud seemed to make it difficult.

"I know a jaguar when I hear one," said Oliveira, doing his best to turn as well. Pedrinho let out another growl. This time it was deeper.

"It's a big one," said Oliveira.

Pedrinho darted along the riverbank and dropped into the water. Oliveira stared at the rustling branches and hissed, "It's coming this way!"

I put my hand over my mouth to stop myself laughing.

"It's one of the boys, you fool!" said Batista.

But Oliveira was in a panic. He pointed his pistol into the bushes and fired. The barrel of his gun flashed yellow and the metallic smell came drifting on the air as he emptied five, then six bullets into the undergrowth.

There was silence for a time as the men made their way back to the edge of the river, still scanning the darkness with their torches. Rain drummed on the water and I waited.

Pedrinho came up for air half-way across the river. He was swimming for the hideout. I don't know if one of the policemen heard him, or if it was just chance but one of the torch beams swooped across the river towards his head. I wanted to call out to warn him. But he must have sensed danger because he disappeared under the water again and the light only picked out the faint swirl in the water where he had been. Moments later, he was alongside me, lying safe in the dark shadows of the beach.

Then the worst possible thing happened. Lightning flashed. Everything was turned to white light and sharp black shadows. And the policemen saw Pedrinho and me lying in the sand.

20 You Don't Fool Me

Thunder cracked.

"There!" yelled Batista, and, at once, the two of them were sloshing towards us along the edge of the river.

We got to our feet. But, as we did, an extraordinary rumbling sound came from the river.

"You don't fool me with your silly animal sounds!" called Batista, plunging on through the water. But it wasn't Pedrinho this time. I saw a dark shape ahead of the men in the shallows of the river and, a moment later, there was an almighty bang. It was like a gun going off. But it wasn't a bullet. It was an alligator smacking its head into the water.

"Amarela!" whispered Pedrinho, wrinkling up his nose.

What happened next I'll never quite know. The

two men seemed to throw themselves backwards at the sight of the alligator's gaping jaws. I saw Amarela's tail snake and thrash through the water.

Oliveira managed to keep his feet but Batista went plunging backwards with an angry grunt and disappeared under the water. Amarela raised her head again and hissed with all her strength. For a moment the air seemed full of her teeth. Batista surfaced a few paces further up stream. Both he and Oliveira were sloshing backwards away from Amarela and Batista was pointing his pistol straight at her head.

I heard Pedrinho say, "No!" and run towards the men. As he ran, he was caught by the alligator's tail, lifted up into the rain and dashed back down into the river. But the gunshot never came. I can only guess Batista's pistol was so full of water it couldn't fire. I saw

Pedrinho lamely struggle to his feet in the wake of
the great snaking tail, and Amarela's teeth glint in
the rain as she closed in on the two policemen.
Then from nowhere a rope fell out of the sky.

It was Alberto on the far bank. The loop of his
lasso landed with a thud round both men and
they were yanked backwards into the middle of
the river. They struggled but the rope held them
and, in no time, Alberto was dragging them into
the shallow water across the river.

That was when I heard Luis coming across the
muddy grass and Mum's voice as well. "Wait
Luis!" she called. "There are dangerous animals in
there!"

"Yes," said Luis, "And I'm going to help catch
two of them!"

With that he leaped out of the
shadows and into the river
where he helped pin the
furious policemen down.
Within moments
Alberto had the two men
bound firmly together
by the arms.

My only disappointment was that Mum didn't swing the bag of piranha fish at Sergeant Batista again. Instead a strange silence fell. Amarela had disappeared. And I waded out across the river to help Pedrinho over to the other side.

He was quite badly hurt. The tail had caught him on one side of his chest and his ribs were heavily bruised. But he didn't complain and, in any case, we soon had plenty of help. Toucan had heard the gunshots and come riding across the farm to see what was happening. And, not long after him, the state police Luis had called for finally arrived.

Mum looked at Alberto's arm and said that he'd been lucky. The bullet had cut the skin, but not touched the bone. Alberto said he'd be fine on two conditions. First, he wanted Batista, Oliveira and the animal skins off the farm. That was easily arranged. The policemen handcuffed Batista and Oliveira and led them away. I gave the keys of the barn to Toucan who said he'd help them load up the skins.

"What's the second thing you want Alberto?" asked Mum, wrapping a makeshift bandage round his arm.

"A cup of coffee," said Alberto. I looked at Pedrinho and he knew why. He looked back at me for a moment then said, "You can have coffee right here."

"What do you mean?" asked Luis.

"I've got a secret hideout over there. Come and see."

Mum, of course, didn't want to cross the river. But Luis said he'd waded through it plenty of times when he was younger and offered to take her on his shoulders. They nearly toppled over in the middle, but they looked pleased with themselves when they got to the other side.

Pedrinho led us into the hideout, and soon we were all drinking sweet coffee round the fire.

"So this is where you've been sloping off to," said Mum. "Did you know about this place, Alberto?"

Alberto sipped his coffee. Then he gave a little shrug and said, "I've known about it for the last year and a half. In fact, I sometimes stop and make myself a coffee down here if Pedrinho's not looking."

Pedrinho's mouth gaped and everyone rocked with laughter.

21 Chumpf

The next morning I woke with the sun and the sounds of the animals. I packed my stuff, ready to leave, and put on my Brazil football shirt for the journey. Pedrinho was waiting in the yard. We had agreed to go down to the hideout one last time before Mum, Luis and I headed for the airport. Monkeys were howling off in the trees and the sky was full of whoops and squawks. When we got to the hideout, Preto was there with his dark tail curled lazily in the sand. But there was no sign of Amarela.

As we sat down near him in the sand, I noticed a sharp pain in one of my toes. I kicked off my trainers and looked. There was something small and black under the skin.

"Is it a *bicho de pé*?" I asked, holding my foot out to Pedrinho.

Pedrinho held my ankle and looked carefully at the toe.

"It's three *bichos de pé*," he said.

I tried to grab my foot back but Pedrinho wouldn't let me. He looked at my face and laughed with his eyes. Then he reached down, squeezed at my toe and held up a black slither.

"A splinter," he said.

I pulled back my foot. He held up a finger and looked round. All I could see was a couple of parrots flying from tree to tree. Then there was a stirring in the dark water and out came Amarela's great, dark head. She growled fiercely and lumbered out of the water on her powerful webbed feet. Pedrinho walked up to her and pulled up his T-shirt to show her his bruised ribs.

"Look what you did to me last night!" he said, squatting down in the sand beside her. Then he looked round and said, "Come closer."

I moved towards them, walking slowly and looking straight at Amarela. Although her face seemed angry, her eyes were calm. I squatted down in front of her.

Her tail gave a flick but she did not move.

"You can touch her if you want," said Pedrinho.

I reached out a hand and wiggled my fingers. Amarela stared. Her mouth hung open, showing her crooked teeth. Some were fat and round, others were tiny and sharp as splinters. I tried to think of something to say but my mind was blank. She backed away a fraction.

"Uh-uh," I said putting my hand just above her head. "I just want to say goodbye, my friend."

Amarela narrowed her eyes a little. Then she made a little sound from somewhere inside her belly. I heard Preto back away behind me. Amarela blinked. I tapped the ground in front of her. Amarela edged forwards a fraction and her yellow eyes looked at me. They were full of tiny specs like stars in the sky. I put out the flat of my hand and touched her side. The skin was bumpy and cool. It was softer than I thought it would be, but I could feel the thickness of the muscles underneath. I squeezed her front leg and she let out a little 'chumpf' sound.

"She likes you," nodded Pedrinho.

Soon after, we headed back.

I said goodbye to the alligators and ducked into the tunnel after Pedrinho.

When I took off my Brazil shirt to cross the river,

I said to Pedrinho, "You can have this."

He didn't say anything. He just took the shirt and smiled. But later, as we came out of the trees near the barn, I felt him slip something into the pocket of my shorts.

"For you," he said.

I could see the pick-up bumping towards us from the farmhouse. It was Alberto, Luis and Mum with all the bags and suitcases in the back.

"Come on, Ant," said Luis, opening the door. "We've been waiting for you."

I looked at my friend, put an arm round his shoulders and said, "Goodbye, Pedrinho."

"Goodbye, my friend, Mr English," he said.

Then he smiled and added, "See … zou … later … alligat-or."

I got into the pick-up beside Mum. As we bumped away I looked in the wing mirror and saw Pedrinho's shaved head bobbing along as he ran after us up the dirt track.

"One day you'll have to come and visit us again, Mr English," said Alberto.

I nodded and put my hand into the pocket of my shorts to see what was there. It was three palm nuts.